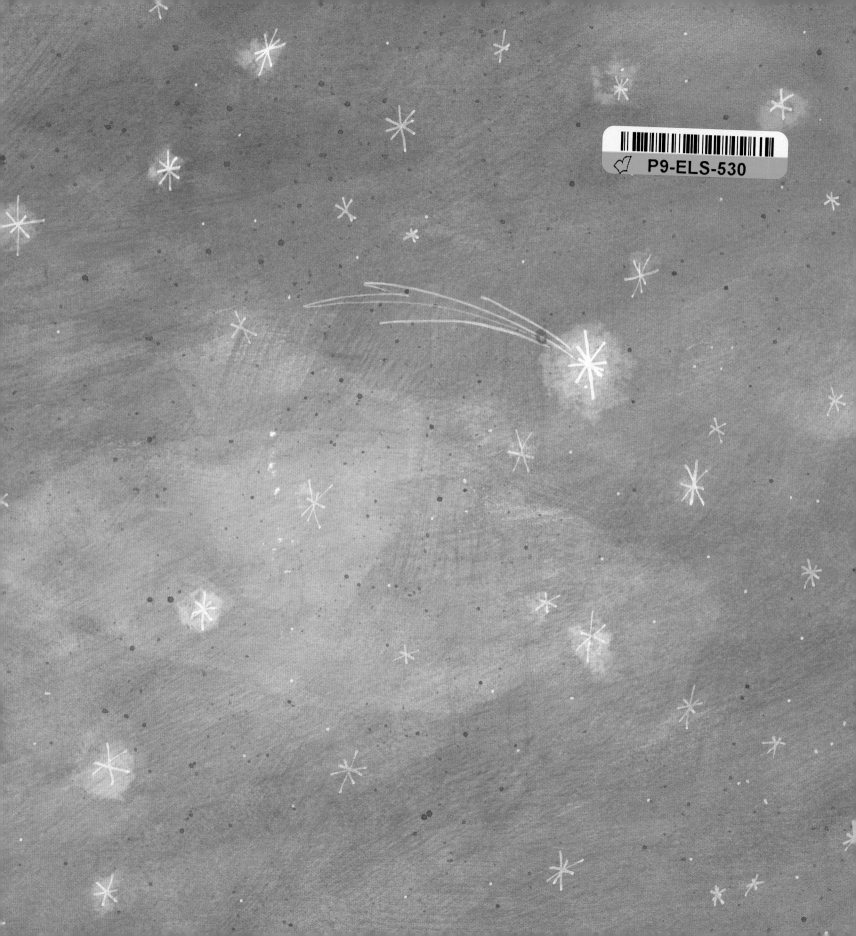

Superluminous

Written and Illustrated by
Ian De Haes

annick press
toronto • berkeley

Superlumineuse by Ian De Haes
Copyright © 2018 Alice Éditions

North American English edition published as *Superluminous*, Annick Press, 2020

Annick Press Ltd.

Library and Archives Canada Cataloguing in Publication

Title: Superluminous / written and illustrated by Ian De Haes.
Other titles: Superlumineuse. English
Names: De Haes, Ian, author, illustrator.
Description: Translation of: Superlumineuse.
Identifiers: Canadiana (print) 20190165898 | Canadiana (ebook) 20190166037 | ISBN 9781773213804
   (hardcover) | ISBN 9781773213835 (PDF) | ISBN 9781773213828 (Kindle) | ISBN 9781773213811 (HTML)
Classification: LCC PQ2704.E22 S8713 2020 | DDC 843/.92—dc23

Published in the U.S.A. by Annick Press (U.S.) Ltd.
Distributed in Canada by University of Toronto Press.
Distributed in the U.S.A. by Publishers Group West.

Printed in China

annickpress.com
iandehaes.com

Also available as an e-book. Please visit annickpress.com/ebooks for more details.

For Mila and Iris,
my superluminous girls

Nour was born luminous.

She glows.

She sparkles.

As though a little sun was
shining right inside of her.

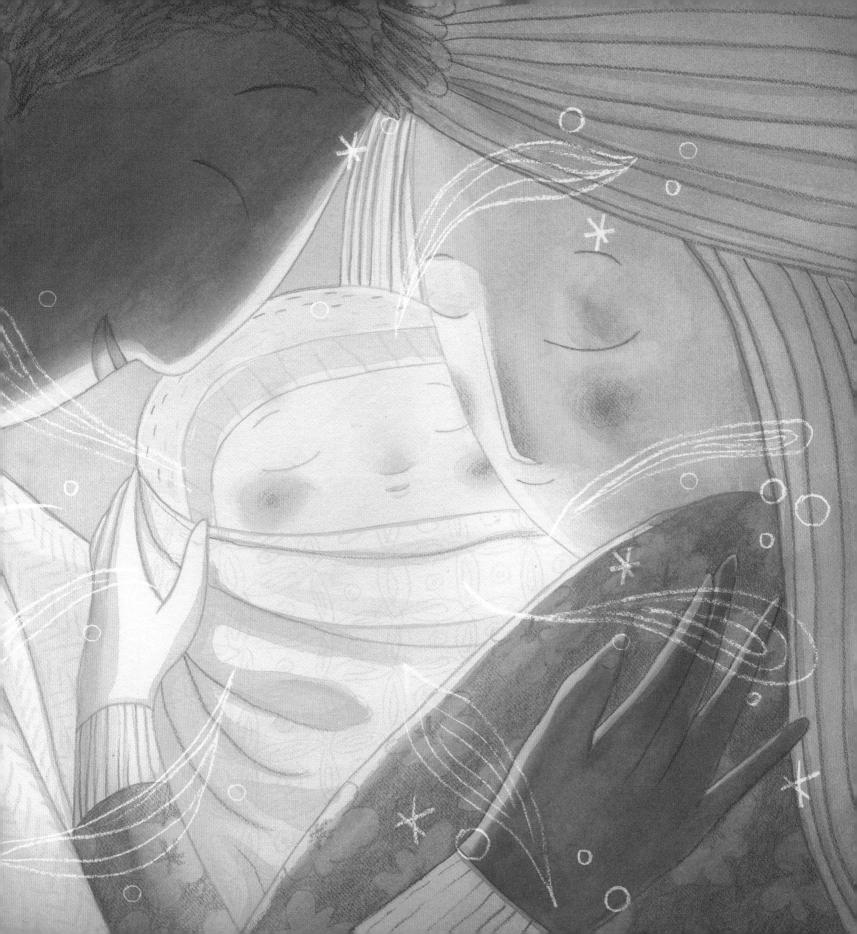

Nour loves her glowing light.

It makes her feel special, even extraordinary!

She spends her days exploring the
darkest, dreariest corners of her house.

Her favorite spot is the attic, where she faces
down all the monsters and ghosts that hide there.

She loves looking at the stars.

Nour sometimes feels like she's one of them—
twinkling, sparking, but a little bit lost in such a big universe.

When there are lots of people around, Nour feels uncomfortable.

She's not sure what's expected of her.

Nour prefers to be alone.

She loves to read stories in bed, cozy and warm—especially stories about superheroes.

Today is Nour's first day of school.

She picks out her best clothes. Even if she's a bit scared, Nour's excited to meet all the other kids, and to show them her beautiful glowing light.

She's certain they will be impressed.

And sure enough, as soon as she gets to school, she is the center of attention.

"How do you do that?" Younès asks.

"I don't know, I was just born this way," Nour explains. "It's kind of a superpower."

"Have you ever saved anyone? Like a real superhero?" Chloe asks.

"Real superheroes have cool outfits," Benjamin, who seems to know about these things, tells her. "Where's yours?"

"Can you turn down your light?" Lucy asks. "It's hurting my eyes."

"Glowing is not a real superpower," Lea decides. "Real superheroes can fly, or pass through walls, or are really strong— like me. Glowing, that's no big deal."

Nour tells herself that Lea is just jealous but wonders if she's also a little bit right.

It's true, Nour thinks. *I'm not that special.*
I'm not super strong.
I'm not super fast.
I'm not super funny.
All I know how to do is shine, like an old lightbulb.
If only I had real superpowers!

Heading home after school,
Nour doesn't feel very well.
It feels like everyone is watching her.

Nobody sees anything special about me,
she thinks to herself. *Even with my light.*

Nour doesn't want to shine bright
anymore. She wishes she were invisible.

For the rest of the week, Nour wears thick, heavy clothes that don't let her light get through. She even covers her hands with gloves and her head with a hat.

She doesn't want anyone looking at her. She doesn't want anyone talking about her. She doesn't want anyone to even notice her.

She makes herself so unremarkable that people forget about her glow.

Now she's completely invisible.

One night, Nour notices that her light is almost out.
All that's left is a little tiny flame, somewhere deep inside
of her. It's very hard to see.

Oh well, Nour thinks, *this light wasn't any good anyway.*

But at the same time, it feels strange. Nour has never
been afraid of the dark, but now the night surrounding
her feels so . . . big.

As she tries to fall asleep, Nour hears crying in the
bedroom next door. Her little sister. She cries louder and
louder. *As loud as a dragon*, Nour thinks.

She knows it's because her sister is afraid of the dark, too.

Nour gets up and tiptoes softly into her sister's room. Nour's glow is not very bright, but she can still use it to see in the dark, like a night-light.

It's enough that when her sister notices it, she calms down. Nour climbs into her sister's crib and hugs her close.

If she could give her light to her sister, to keep her from being scared, Nour would.

The two sisters fall asleep, snuggled together, calm and quiet.

The next morning, Nour's parents are dazzled
to find their two daughters together in the crib.

Nour rubs her sleepy eyes and realizes that
her light hasn't gone away—it's grown!

And her sister is glowing, too!

Nour is so happy.

She understands now that she can share her light—it's no longer something she has to carry on her own.

She doesn't want to hide it anymore. She wants to light up all the little sisters and brothers in the world, so nobody is ever scared again.

Maybe she's a superhero after all!

Nour gives her mom and dad a hug and they start to glow, too.

Nour leaves for school brighter than ever.

She realizes that just by looking people in the eye, and smiling as she passes them, she can share her superpower.

She really is

Superluminous!

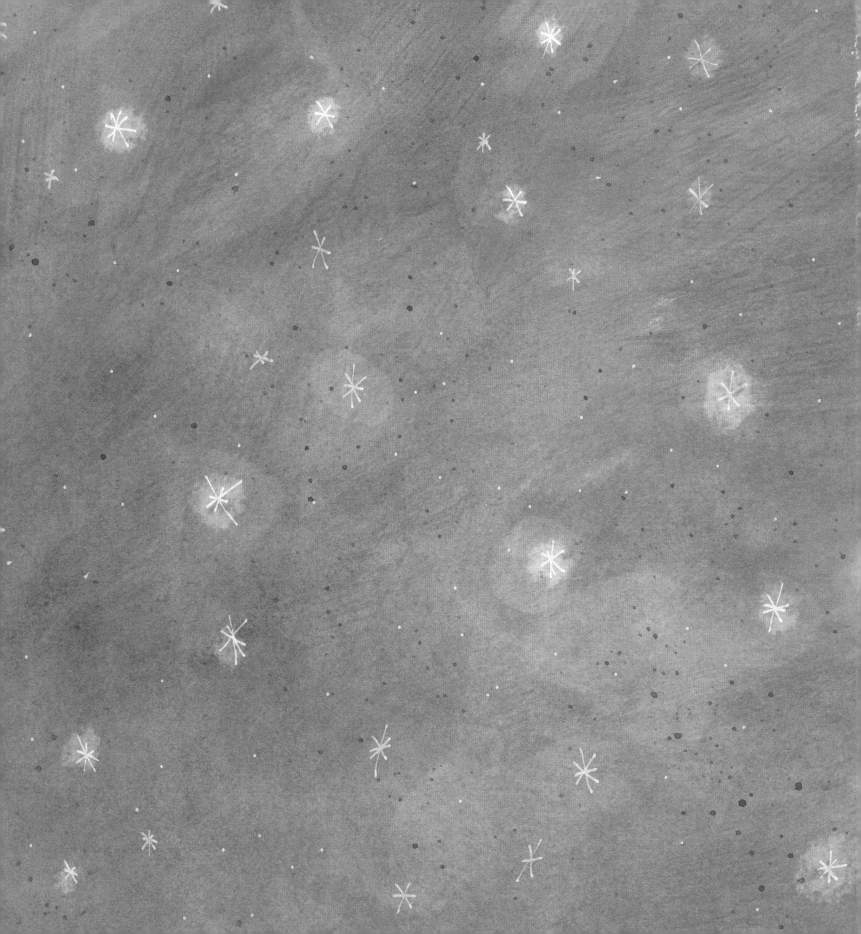